YANA
[You Are Not Alone]

by Amy Klco

Maddie,
You are NEVER alone!
Amy Klco

Enchantment Press
YANA: You Are Not Alone
Amy Klco

Copyright © 2016 by Amy Klco
All Rights Reserved

Cover Design by Louisa Firethorne

Published in the United States by Enchantment Press
www.enchantmentpress.com

ISBN 978-0-9979511-6-5

RL: 3.0

This book is dedicated to Serra Barr,
who inspired the idea in the first place,
and to all my former students,
my future students,
and ALL students
who struggle.

Remember, you are not alone!

Trigger Warning
(Otherwise known as Disclaimer)

This book is written to help shed light on some of the struggles that students face every day. The characters and specific events in this book are fictitious—the emotional effects events like these can cause are, sadly, all too real. If reading this book brings up emotional issues for you or anyone you know, please seek help. Healing can only come when you admit you need it. By asking for help, you will discover that you are not alone.

If you or someone you know is struggling with depression or suicidal thoughts, please call or text the National Suicide Prevention Hotline at 9-8-8.

Jacob North

How did I end up here? I'm a good kid, the kind who never gets into any trouble, right? I made it all the way to my junior year of high school without ever getting so much as a detention. So what am I doing in the principal's office? Why was my dad called in? Why are they talking about expelling me? Me, of all people? I do my work. I get good grades. I don't get in any trouble with anyone. In fact, most of the time, nobody even seems to notice I'm alive. But now, suddenly, everyone seems interested in me, in what I'm thinking, in what I'm going through. They never seemed to care before. Why are they so interested now?

"Do you understand why you are here, Jacob?" the principal, Mr. Jones, asks me.

What can I say? Yes. No. I mean, I understand that what I did is "wrong." What I don't really get is why everyone is making such a big deal about it. All I did was write down my thoughts, those thoughts that nobody ever cared enough to find out about before. All those years of being quiet, sitting all alone with my eyes lowered, hoping no one would notice me, and yet praying, deep inside, that they would, even just a little. Hoping that someone would notice my pain. That maybe somebody, somewhere, could help.

This is not the type of help I was looking for. And that is not the type of answer Mr. Jones wants from me.

"He asked you a question," my dad reminds me. "Answer him," he adds, as if I didn't know, as if I needed him to tell me what to do, just as he always does.

It's his way of showing his love, I guess. Since Mom left, back when I was six, he's done his best to be a father to me, but I don't think he has any idea how. He never really was a dad to me before she left. When Mom was still around, he was always too busy to even pay much attention to me. Or Mom, for that matter. Which is why she left. I understand that. What I don't understand is why she left without me. And why Dad thinks he now has to tell me what to do.

"Yes," I say quietly, meekly. "I shouldn't have done what I did. But I didn't mean for the note to be found. It was just for me, just to help me to..."

"We understand," Ms. Birch, my teacher, jumps in. "I didn't bring the note to Mr. Jones because of what you said about me. I'm really more concerned about what you wrote about yourself."

"Still, there are consequences for what you wrote," Mr. Jones pipes up. It bothers him, I think, when someone else tries to take control of the situation. He is the principal, the law of the land, so to speak. And no one is going to upstage him. "It clearly states in the student handbook that 'students are not allowed to abuse or make threats to teachers or any staff of this school.' This is not something I can ignore, Jacob. I have to take action."

"What exactly did he write?" my dad asks.

Mr. Jones shuffles through the papers on his desk before he finds the one he's looking for. "Here," he says after a minute, holding up a piece of lined paper in his hand. "It says, 'I hate Ms. Birch so much! Doesn't she realize how hard I worked on that report? And yet, she gave me an F, just because I didn't have an outline with it. Really? Her name shouldn't be Ms. Birch, it should be Ms. Bi....'" Mr. Jones stopped reading. "Um, yeah, well, let's see... he goes on to write, 'I want to kill her. I want to stab Ms. Birch in the heart and...oh, wait. She doesn't have a heart!' But then he goes on to talk about himself. He says..."

My dad cuts him off. "I don't care what he has to say about himself! I care about this!" Then he turns to me. "Why would you write something like that? Haven't I raised you better than that?"

I thought about answering him. No. He hasn't

raised me at all. The only reason he is pretending to care about any of this is because it makes him look bad. People might think he's a bad parent or something.

"I asked you a question," my dad screams in my face. "Talk to me, you little…" He stops just in time, remembering that there are others in the room. He saves the yelling and the swear words for when we are alone. They don't help his image as a "good dad."

"I think we need to talk about what he wrote about himself," Ms. Birch interjects. "He wrote here, 'I don't want to be alive. I shouldn't be here. Nobody cares about me and I should just…'"

My dad just laughs. "Nobody cares about him? Why would he say that? I'm here, aren't I? Obviously I care. He's just doing this to get attention."

Am I? I wonder. *Well, if I am, I guess my plan worked. I'm getting all the attention I could ever want, now. More than I ever wanted. Now I just want to go back to being invisible.*

"Be that as it may," Mr. Jones jumps in again, "the student handbook clearly states that, if we feel that a student is a 'threat to themselves or others,' they can not be in school. I'm afraid there is nothing we can do. Jacob will be suspended from school until we can have a Code of Conduct meeting. Then we'll decide if he will be expelled or not."

"And how long will that take?" my father asks, impatiently.

"The meeting will be on Friday afternoon, around four o'clock. I'm sorry for any inconvenience this may cause you, but..."

"Like hell you are," my father mumbles under his breath. Either Mr. Jones doesn't hear him, or he pretends not to, because he just continues with what he's saying.

"Now, I'm sorry, but I really do need to get some work done. If you'll excuse me..." Mr. Jones stands up and ushers us all out of his office.

"So what is he supposed to do with this time off?" my dad asks Ms. Birch as we stand outside the office. "Can he get the work he's going to miss? I don't want him to get behind in his classes because of this."

Ms. Birch shakes her head sadly, almost like she really cares. "I'm sorry. The policy is that they can't make up any schoolwork when they are out of school for suspension. But..." she perks up a little. "I can give Jacob a little project to work on while he's off." She smiles, like she just came up with a great idea. "Jacob," she says directly to me. "I would like you to write a paper for me, okay? Like a letter. I want you to do some reflection and tell me why you wrote that note. Maybe if you figure out why you did it, it will help you to not do it again. Okay?"

Is she serious? Really? I could tell her why I did it, in four words. I. Hate. This. School! I hate the teachers. I hate the principal. I hate the kids. I hate everything about this school. Even myself. Especially myself.

"I think that sounds like a great idea," I hear

my dad saying. "That will give him something to keep him busy while I'm at work. I can read over it when he's done and make sure everything is spelled right before he hands it in." He says it as if he is very proud of himself for the offer, as if it's a huge sacrifice on his part, but he's willing to do it because he's such a great dad. Give me a break!

I don't say any of this, of course. I just smile. Not a happy smile or a smile like I'm thinking of something funny. This is the type of smile I give when I'm really upset about something, but I know there's nothing I can do about it. Like when Brandon stole my homework last month in math class, put his name on it, and turned it in. The teacher didn't even notice it wasn't his handwriting. She just gave him my A and I got a 0. And all I could do was smile. She wouldn't have listened if I tried to tell her the truth. Teachers never do. No one ever does.

"Okay," Ms. Birch replies with a smile, one probably as fake as my own. "Why don't you walk

Jacob down to his locker to get anything he might need? Hopefully we'll see him back here real soon."

"He'll have that paper done by the end of the week," my dad tells her. "I'll bring it to you myself." Again, his voice reflects what a huge sacrifice this will be on his part.

"Oh, no rush," Ms. Birch replies. "Whenever he gets it done."

"He'll have it done by Friday morning," my dad repeats. Then he guides me out of the office.

We don't even stop by my locker. "There's nothing you need in there anyway," he tells me. "If they're not going to let you do your work, there's no point in getting anything. Let's get out of this place."

I don't mention to my dad about the one important thing that is in my locker: the latest story I'm writing. I doubt he'd understand why I would need that.

Dad doesn't really say anything to me when

we get home. He doesn't talk to me that much, anyway. This is one time when I'm glad of it.

We eat dinner in silence. When we're done, he says, "I want you to get started on that paper tonight. You will have it done by Friday." Then he stands up and goes to his room to watch the game. We have a TV in the living room, but I don't really know why. He always goes to his room, to *his* TV, to watch his sports. He says he doesn't want to be interrupted when he's trying to pay attention to something important. Obviously, I am not one of those things.

After he leaves, I think about turning on the TV myself. But he told me to write that paper, and he'll yell if he hears the TV on. Plus, there's nothing I really want to watch, anyway.

There's nothing I want to do, either, except maybe just break down and cry. But I can't do that. Even with his TV going, he'd hear that as well. I used to cry a lot when I was younger. I don't know why: I was just an emotional kid. Every time

I started, Dad would tell me to "stop crying like a little girl" and "be a man." Then he'd swat me upside the head. It was never very hard, but it was enough to make me want to cry even more. If I did, he'd do it again, harder.

I don't cry much anymore. At least, not so that anyone can hear me. My tears stay inside now.

Since there's nothing else to do, I pull out some paper to write that stupid letter to Ms. Birch. Why the hell would she ask me to write about why I wrote that note? I'm not the one who doesn't understand. It's them. All of them. Those wise adults who think they know everything, but who don't really know anything at all. They don't see what's really happening all around them. They don't see what I see; they don't know what I know.

"So tell them," a voice inside my head says. No, I'm not crazy. But I swear it's like there was someone else talking to me at that moment. Or maybe just another part of me. "They want to know why you wrote that note. So tell them. Tell them why. Who knows, they might just listen for once."

"Fine," I tell the voice. "But watch out!"

Dear Ms. Birch, I write.

You want to know why I wrote that note? Okay, I'll tell you. But I want you to ask yourself this: Do you really want to know? Can you handle hearing the truth, the whole depressing truth about what school is really like? Because if you can't handle the truth, you'd better stop reading right now.

I write that much quickly, without much thought. But then I stop. Where should I start? With the paper Ms. Birch gave me an F on? No, that's not where this started.

Maybe it started the first day I walked into her class, with the look she gave me when she first saw me. She looked me up and down, taking in my holey jeans, my black sweatshirt, my hair that hung in my face, dyed at the tips. She was sizing me up, forming an opinion of me within the first few seconds of meeting me. She gave me a friendly smile, but I was left wondering what she really thought. Did she, like all my teachers, write me off as "one of those kids" before she even knew me?

Is that where I should start this story?

No. That wasn't the start, either. I had to go back further. This isn't just about me and Ms. Birch. This started the first day I went to school... when I was in preschool. I'll start there.

School is not, as adults would like to believe, a great place for children. For some children, it might be fine. For the clever ones, the "good" ones, the pretty ones, the ones whose parents are on the PTO. But for the rest of us...

When I started school, I was small for my age. And shy. I would cry a lot. And sometimes, I would wet myself. None of this helped me make friends. Even in preschool, kids knew who the easy targets were, the ones they could pick on to make themselves feel better. And I was as easy as they come.

I still remember the first time I peed my pants in school. It wasn't my fault. The teacher said we could only use the bathroom twice a day: once in the morning and once after snack. Some kids were fooling around, making a mess in the bathroom instead of doing what they were supposed to. Ms. Ruth didn't know who was doing it, so we all had to pay the price.

I couldn't help it if I had to go. I tried to get Ms. Ruth's attention, but she was too busy working with another kid. She didn't even see me standing next to her...until it was too late. Brandon Collins was the first to notice. I will never forget that moment. "Look at Jacob!" he cried. "Jacob peed his pants! What a baby!"

"Baby, baby!" the kids all started chanting in unison. I think it was the first time the whole class was focused on the same thing at the same time: me. And, as any four-year-old would do when everyone was laughing at them, I started to cry. That just made things ten times worse.

I'll say this for Ms. Ruth, though. She was nice about it. She told me it was okay, and she walked me down to the office so they could call my mom to come bring a change of clothes.

That was when Mom was still with us. When she came, she gave me a big hug (even though I was wet) and helped me change into my clean clothes in the staff bathroom. Then she sent me back to class. I never told her what the kids had said. I was afraid that she would worry about me. I guess I didn't have to be. She clearly didn't worry about me when she left.

Laura Birch

By the time I finally get home from school after a long day of teaching, my mind is a jumble. More than normal, even. I feel so bad about what happened to Jacob. That's not what I wanted. I don't care if he makes threats about me. He's just a teen, struggling as best he can to get through the day. He was mad. And maybe he had a right to be. After all, he did write a good paper. Why did I ever make that rule about having an outline? It's silly. I don't even use an outline when I write. Who cares what we were taught this summer in that great "How to Teach Writing" training? I know better. Why didn't I act like it?

So I found the note and I knew why he wrote it. Heck, I wrote my share of notes like that back when I was in school. I could have just ignored it, thrown it away and pretended I never saw it. Then things would be just fine.

Except, of course, if they weren't. I'm not worried about threats from Jacob. But I am worried about Jacob. Because of what he said about himself. Because of how he feels about himself. Because I've been there, too.

I guess I could have just clipped out the part I was concerned about, the part about him, and never even shown Mr. Jones the rest. Why hadn't I thought of that earlier?

After tossing and turning for hours, unable to sleep, I finally give up trying. I get out of bed, go into my silent living room, and settle down in my recliner with a pad of paper. I told Jacob that he needed to write about why he'd written that note. But now, I feel like I should be the one to write, to write to him and explain why I turned it in. Why, above all, I didn't mean to hurt him. Somehow, I need to show him that he isn't alone.

Dear Jacob, I start.

I want you to know that I am very sorry about what happened. I didn't mean to get you into trouble. All I wanted to do was help you.

You may not believe this, but I understand how you're feeling. I was there once, myself. School was not always easy for me.

In kindergarten, I was a very quiet girl. And when I was little, I had a blanket that I took with me everywhere. My parents thought that I should leave it at home when I went to school, but I refused. I didn't know, yet, how mean kids could be. I learned pretty quickly.

At first, they just laughed at me and teased me about it. Then Thomas Dillon decided it would be funny to take it from me and hide it.

I can still remember it like it was yesterday. It was free time. I set my blanket down next to me as I looked through the cool books that Ms. Simmons had in her classroom. I was engaged at looking at the pictures of frogs and lizards and snakes, so engaged that I must not have noticed when Thomas snuck up behind me and quietly drug my blanket away. It wasn't until Ms. Simmons said that free time was over and that we had to return to our seats that I realized that Blankey wasn't with me. I looked all around. Where could it have gone? Then I noticed the other kids giggling and pointing at me.

"What happened to that dumb old blanket?" Thomas asked me, and all the other kids broke out into laughter.

I was so angry. "What did you do with it?" I asked him. "If you took it, I'll..." I never got a chance to tell Thomas what I would do, because Ms. Simmons stepped in.

"Thomas, do you know where Laura's blanket is?" she asked.

Thomas shrugged. "How should I know?" he replied.

"Thomas?" Ms. Simmons looked hard at him. "Do I have to call your mother?"

We were at the age where that was still a real threat. Thomas confessed. "I put it in the boys bathroom," he said. "It's just a joke. I don't know what the big deal is."

I ran to the bathroom before he could even finish talking, not even caring that I was a girl going into the boys bathroom. Then I saw it–floating in the toilet. And it wasn't the only thing floating in there.

I sat down right there and cried and cried. Nobody could get me to stop. Finally, they had to call my mom to come get me–and my blanket. (She brought a plastic bag to put it in.)

She washed my blanket several times, just to make sure it was clean. But it never was the same after that. And I don't think I was, either. It was my first real experience with how cruel kids could be. It wouldn't be my last.

Jacob North

I try going to sleep early, because after all, what else is there to do? But I just can't. It's not working. My mind is swimming with memories I can't ignore, things I just have to write about. There's so much I want to tell somebody, anybody, I realize. Now, I finally have somebody who just might be willing to listen. If Ms. Birch is willing to hear my stories, then I'll tell them. All of them. So instead of trying to sleep, I get up and start writing again.

I enjoyed kindergarten, I write. But first grade was hard for me. That was when they started expecting me to sit still and do my work. I tried to, I really did, but I would get wiggly. I needed to talk, to share what I knew.

I needed to move. And sometimes, as my arms and legs were flying around me, they would hit other kids. I didn't mean to, but...

I got into a lot of trouble that year, because I just couldn't behave like the teacher wanted me to. She wanted me to be like the good kids, like Hope, who was always doing exactly what she was told, raising her hand when she wanted to say something, listening quietly when the teacher was talking. Me, I would just yell out when I knew the answer. Or I'd get out of my seat to go sharpen my pencil or get some paper or to see what another student had on their desk...

When I got in trouble, the teacher would take away my recess. Didn't she understand? I needed to run and jump and move. If I couldn't do that even during recess, how was I supposed to get through the rest of the day?

"Jacob," she said one day, when I was standing by the fence while all the other kids were playing. "Why do you keep getting into so much trouble? Can't you just stay still and keep your hands to yourself?"

"I feel like I can't get my energy out," I tried to explain.

"I spin around because I can't get all the wigglies out."

"Well, I can't have you spinning around in my class all the time. You have got to learn to control those wigglies or I'll have to call your parents."

Even as a kid, I knew that didn't even make sense. How were they going to get me to control myself when I couldn't do it on my own? Besides, they were too busy fighting to worry about me. If my teacher called them, it would just make things worse.

In the end, my parents did help me control myself, to not be moving all the time. But not in the way that my teacher hoped. And not in the way that I wanted them to.

My mom left in December of that year. Merry Christmas. They told me later that they tried to stay together until after the holidays, for me. But they just couldn't do it. Mom moved out on December 21st. That was the last time I ever saw her. She called me that Christmas day, and every Christmas since then, but that's the only time I hear from her. She is like a stranger to me now. And what do I have to say to a stranger?

Since that day, I have not been burdened with too

much energy. I've had other issues to deal with, but being too happy and excited is not one of them. Not anymore.

Laura Birch

Today at school, I'm giving a test. Thank goodness, because I don't feel much like teaching. I know that sounds awful, but I am human. Some days, I just don't have the energy for standing up on that stage called the front of the class. Some days, I wish I were sitting in the student's chair, staring blankly at someone else instead.

Besides, today my mind is too much inside myself. This thing with Jacob has really got me thinking. It's like I can't stop, I can't shut my mind off and focus on the students I have in front of me. So as they take their test, I pull out a blank paper and continue my letter. There's still so much to say.

Second grade was when my troubles really started, I tell Jacob in the letter. That was when my inability to read started to show. Until then, I struggled a bit, but all my teachers kept saying, "She'll pick it up soon. Some kids just take longer to learn to read than others." But by second grade, it was clear to all of us that I wasn't going to just "pick it up." I tried. But they wanted me to sit still and stare at letters that seemed to jump around when I looked at them. None of it made any sense, no matter how many times the teacher told me to sound it out.

I knew what the problem was—or at least I thought I did. It was very simple: I was stupid. And the rest of the kids in my class just reinforced what I already believed. They laughed at me and called me names.

In second grade, kids aren't supposed to know bad words, right? Or so adults like to pretend. But someone did. They saw my last name and realized how close it was to another word. Before long, the whole school was calling me "Laura Bitch."

That started the jokes about me being a dog. I heard

a lot of barking noises. One kid even brought in a can of dog food and left it on my desk for lunch.

The other kids might have been too young to really understand what that word meant, but they knew it was a bad word, and they knew it hurt me when they called me it. What else was there to know?

Jacob North

Dad wakes me up before he leaves for work the next morning. "You don't get to sleep in just because you got yourself kicked out of school for a while," he tells me. "You've got chores you need to get done. And there's the paper you have to write for that teacher. I want that done by Friday morning. You understand?"

I nod. I could tell him I already started working on it. I could promise to work on writing it all day. But it doesn't matter what I say. His reply will be the same: "Just get it done." I don't need to actually go through the conversation to know how it will turn out. It always turns out the same.

Honestly, though, I don't really mind having to

write this letter. I have a lot I still want to say, a lot I need to say.

Third grade was a strange year for me, I write once Dad finally leaves. That's the year I was friends with Brandon Collins. (Yes, the Brandon who made fun of me when I peed my pants in preschool.)

I'm not sure exactly why we became friends. I guess because Brandon wanted to be. He'd probably gone through all his other possible friends and I was just the next one on the list. Brandon had a tendency to go through friends pretty quick. That should have been a warning for me, but of course, it wasn't. I didn't stop to think about why Brandon wanted to be my friend. I just knew that he was cool and that if I was his friend, that meant that I was cool, too.

But there was a price to pay. As I quickly learned, being cool meant being mean: you had to pick on those who were not cool. That's what Brandon taught me. And top of our list of "not cool" kids was Hope Morris.

Hope was a very sweet girl, but she always made me

think of a lost puppy. She was always the teacher's pet. If you talked to her at all, she would follow you around for weeks trying to get your attention again. And she would do anything to get you to like her.

Brandon knew that. That's why he gave her that note after class one day. It said on it, "Hope, I really like you. Meet me after school on the playground." Then Brandon signed it with <u>my</u> name.

"What do I do if she shows up?" I asked Brandon.

He shrugged. "See what you can get her to do. I bet she'll kiss you if you ask her to. She'll do anything you ask her to do."

I didn't really want to kiss Hope. I didn't want to kiss any-one. I was still at that stage where I thought girls were "yucky." But I didn't say that to Brandon. If that is what the cool kids did, then that is what I would do, too.

I waited for her after school. Brandon was there, too. He was hiding behind the bushes so she wouldn't see him.

"Hi," she said, looking down. She was pretty cute

when she blushed, I thought. I wasn't so sure I wanted to go through with this plan. If Brandon hadn't been there, I wouldn't have.

"Do you like me?" I asked Hope.

"Yeah," she replied, sheepishly.

"How much?" I asked.

"A lot," she replied, still looking down at the ground.

"Then kiss me," I ordered her.

She leaned forward and closed her eyes. For a minute, I was actually excited about the idea of my first kiss. Then Brandon jumped out of the bushes with a large plastic toy pig. When Hope leaned in to kiss me, Brandon put the pig in the way. Hope's lips fell smack on the pig's pink butt.

"Pig kisser!" Brandon cried, laughing. "Hope is a pig kisser!"

That's when I heard the bushes erupt with laughter. Brandon wasn't the only one hiding in the bushes, apparently. It sounded like the whole third grade class was there.

Hope looked at me, confused. There were tears

forming in her eyes. "What?" she asked me. And then, "Why? I thought you liked me."

Brandon laughed. "How could he like a pig kisser like you?" he asked. "How could anyone like you?"

"Pig kisser!" the voices in the bushes sang out. "Pig kisser," the kids cried as they poured out from the bushes and surrounded her.

Hope turned around and ran, tears running down her cheeks. I just watched her go. I should have gone after her. I should have said I was sorry, that I didn't know what Brandon was planning. But I didn't. Cool kids don't feel bad when they do something funny, right? And obviously it was funny—I could hear everyone laughing.

I probably would have stayed friends with Brandon, despite the things he got me to do when I was with him. I guess I'm glad that he grew tired of me before long. I wasn't any fun, he said. He moved on to someone else and left me alone. And I mean all alone. None of my old friends wanted to talk to me anymore, after the way I'd treated them when I was with him.

That's when I first started writing. Writing became

my only friend. In many ways, it is still my best friend. When no one else is there for me, I can always turn to my writing. Then I don't feel quite so alone.

Laura Birch

I stay late after school, just like I normally do. But this time, it's not to do grading or lesson planning or even to clean the pencil drawings off the desks. Instead, I work on my letter to Jacob. I have more I want to say. For one thing, there's that one day, in fourth grade.

My whole fourth grade year was awful, I write. *All the other kids called me names when the teacher wasn't listening, and worst of all, they would ignore me. I spent so much time on the playground, being ignored by all the other kids, feeling sorry for myself. Except for that one day, the day of the first snow of the year...*

I sat in the middle of the playground that day, quietly

gathering the snow, shaping it into a hill. A little more here, a little more there. Sculpturing a deer, my favorite animal, with the snow. Happy, content for once. Until they started coming to bug me.

"What are you doing all alone?" they asked.

"Are you feeling sorry for yourself?"

"What's wrong with you?"

For months, they ignored me on the playground. Ignored me as I sat on the swings, feeling lonely, feeling sad, wanting to cry. No friends. No one to talk to. No one to hang out with. And they never even noticed I was alone.

But on this day the snow came, and I abandoned my normal habit of sitting on the swings, feeling sorry for myself. Instead, I ran to the open field and became engrossed in my project. I was having fun, enjoying myself. Happy for once.

But they saw me alone—the other kids—and thought I must be lonely. When I was in the crowd, being ignored and miserable, it was okay. But there must be something wrong if I was alone—and happy. Now they had to bug me. Now they were concerned.

"I'm fine," I told them, but they wouldn't believe me. They couldn't understand. How could I be happy by myself? Wouldn't it be better to be with everyone else—ignored, lonely, and miserable?

Jacob North

"So, what did you do all day while I was working?" Dad asks me while we're eating dinner. He always tries to make sure we have a proper "sit-down" dinner. I think he read somewhere that that's what good families do. It's supposed to give families time to talk to each other. Of course, since we never really have anything to say to each other...

When I was little, I tried to get interested in the things he was interested in, which mostly meant sports. I watched the games with him and asked all kinds of questions to understand what was going on. Then he'd yell at me to be quiet so he could pay attention. Before long, I would sneak out of the room and go do my own thing. At least when I was by myself, I wasn't getting yelled at.

"I worked on my letter to Ms. Birch," I tell him.

"Worked on it? You mean you're not done yet? How long does it take to write one little letter?"

I shrug. "I have a lot to say," I reply.

"Well, you'd better start with saying 'I'm sorry.' I still can't believe you would write something like that. As if you were some hoodlum who doesn't know right from wrong. I knew I was being too easy on you."

No one uses the word "hoodlum" anymore, I think, except my dad. But I'm not going to correct him. Only a "hoodlum" would do that...

Dad shakes his head. "Well, you've got two more days to get it done. No excuses."

We eat the rest of the meal in silence. As I said, this "sit-down" dinner idea really is a waste of time.

Honestly, I can't wait for Dad to go up to his room. I want to be alone. I want to do more writing. My story isn't done yet. I want to tell Ms. Birch about Daniel.

Once Dad finally goes upstairs with a "Remember to finish that damn paper," I write more.

I became friends with Daniel during fifth grade. And it was thanks to my writing. I was sitting on the playground, working on my stories like I often did, when he came up to me. He was new to my school. I'd never seen him before. There was something about him that made him seem different from the other boys, but I wasn't sure what it was.

"Hi," he said as he sat down next to me.

"Hi," I replied.

"My name is Daniel," he told me. "Not Dan or Danny, but Daniel."

I nodded my head. "I'm Jacob," I told him. "Not Jake or Jay. And definitely not Cob, like corn-on-the cob." We both laughed.

"What are you doing?" he asked, pointing towards my pad of paper.

"I'm writing a story," I told him with pride. "It's

about a robot that tries to take over the world. And then a superhero comes to save the day."

"Cool," Daniel replied. "You should let me do the pictures for it. I love to draw." I knew, at that moment, that we were going to be friends for life.

I stop writing for a moment and think back to that day, so long ago. It was early spring. The sun was out, but there was still a chill in the air. I can still see Daniel's face, so young and hopeful. The world was before us and we thought that all our dreams could come true. What happened? How did I become so jaded?

Laura Birch

At last I head home to my empty apartment. I never planned on being single, on living by myself. In the dreams I had when I was younger, I had a loving, supportive husband and three darling kids who smiled up at me whenever I came in the room. But life never is like you plan.

In a way, I'm lucky to be able to come to an empty home when I get done with a long day at work. Being around people all day takes its toll on me. I just need quiet time to relax. Read. Play on my computer. Or, like tonight, to write.

Sixth grade was the year—the only year—I was popular, I write to Jacob. *But that's just as well. I learned from* that year that I never wanted to be popular again. It was too much work being someone that I wasn't–and being mean to everyone who wasn't "one of us."

My best friend was Rachel Renee. Or it had been, until Sammy decided that she wanted to be friends with me. Sammy was the most popular girl in class. So of course, if she wanted to be friends with me, that made me popular, too. Whatever she did, I followed along. Even the day we followed Rachel home and made fun of her.

I used to walk home from school every day with Rachel. She lived just around the corner from me. She was the first real friend I ever had. But that didn't stop me from teasing her with Sammy.

She was walking home alone, since I wasn't there to walk with her. Me, Sammy, and a few other girls were hanging out after school when we saw her walk by.

"Hey," Sammy called out to her. "I've got a question for you?"

Rachel stopped and looked at her. "What?" she asked.

"How come you're so ugly?" Sammy asked and we all started to laugh.

Rachel turned around and kept walking.

"I asked you a question," Sammy called after her. "How come you're so ugly?" We all walked over to where she was, surrounding her.

"I don't know," Rachel replied and tried to walk past us.

I stood right in her way. "She asked you a question," I said. "Why are you so ugly, huh? There's got to be a reason."

I will never forget the look she gave me. She looked at me like I had broken her heart. I could see the tears forming in her eyes.

I just gave her a cold stare in return. "Answer the question," I told her.

She shrugged, and I could see that she was now starting to shake. "I guess it's because of my parents," she said, and then turned around and ran off.

Even then, I looked to Sammy first, to see what she would do. Sammy just shrugged, laughed, and said, "What a dumb answer. That girl is dumb and ugly."

We were all called down to the principal's office the next day. But there was no punishment the school could *have given me that was worse than the look in Rachel's eyes that day.*

I still remember that look. It haunts me even now. I see it all the time in the eyes of the students I know are going through the same thing she did. I want to stop it; I want to get rid of all bullying in my school and every school. But what can one teacher do?

Jacob North

"Rise and shine, sleepy-head," my father says at six the next morning. "I've got a whole list of things for you to do today."

"But I'm working on that letter for Ms. Birch," I tell him as I try to adjust my eyes to being open.

"Nonsense. How long does it take to write a silly letter? You're just trying to keep from doing any work. But not anymore. This isn't supposed to be a vacation for you."

"But I..." I start, but then stop myself. I know he wouldn't believe me, anyway.

"No 'buts.' Here's a list of things I want you to get done today."

I look at the list: do the dishes, shovel the snow,

clean out the garage... "I'll never be able to get all this done today," I tell him.

"Never say never," he replies. "I'll see you tonight. And I want to see everything finished by then. Just put your mind to it, stay focused, and you'll have it done in no time." And then just like that, he leaves.

I try to do what he asked me to, at least for a while. I do the dishes and clean up the kitchen. Then I put on my coat and some gloves, pull the snow shovel out of the garage (there's no way that's getting cleaned in one day) and start working on the snow.

I hate winter, I write to Ms. Birch after I get back inside and thaw out a bit. *Not because of the snow, not really. I like the snow, until after Christmas is over. But then it just drags on. Those months from January through March are the worst. Cold. No sunshine. No way to get outside. And slowly, all hope seems to drain away.*

Except for when I was in seventh grade. That was the year I had a "girlfriend." Hope Morris. Yes, the pig kisser, although she'd apparently forgiven me for that incident. Maybe she realized it wasn't my idea. Or maybe she just cared more about having someone–anyone–like her than about holding a grudge. For whatever reason, she passed me a note in math one day that said, "Do you want to be my boyfriend? Yes or no?" I circled "yes," passed it back to her, and that was that.

It was all sweet and innocent. I know some kids were already trying more "grown-up" things at that age, but not us. We barely held hands. And she only kissed me once.

We were at the park by our school one Saturday, playing on the playground equipment like we were little kids again. She was trying to do the monkey bars. Her hand slipped, and she fell. I rushed over and helped her up. As I lifted her to her feet, she leaned in and kissed me. I didn't say anything. I just turned away, embarrassed and confused, and went back to the swings. I wish now that I had said something, anything, to let her know how

I felt about her. Because that was the last time we were happy together.

And it was all because of that kiss.

I thought we were alone that day, in our own little world of happiness. But someone (I never found out who) saw us kiss. By Monday, the news was all over the school. Word of mouth worked at lightning speed when the gossip was good. And what could be better than this? I was spotted kissing the pig-kisser! Which meant, of course, that I must be the pig.

I couldn't go anywhere without hearing someone make "oinking" sounds behind me. I would hear comments like, "I smell bacon" as I passed in the halls. I even had someone ask me if I'd spent the weekend rolling around in the mud.

There wasn't much I could do about it. I tried telling my teachers, but they never heard the comments. The only thing they did was tell me to just ignore them. That if I didn't react to it, they'd stop. Well, guess what? That advice sucks! The more you try to ignore the kids who are picking on you, the harder they try. They won't stop until they get a reaction, which is usually what they get.

Finally, after a long night of prank phone calls saying "The pig says 'oink,'" I knew that there was only one thing I could do. I had to break up with Hope. And it wouldn't be enough to just talk to her quietly and explain why I couldn't be her boyfriend anymore. No. I had to make it public. And I had to make it definite.

I chose the next day, at lunchtime. I was sitting next to Daniel in the lunchroom, squeezed in between a bunch of burping boys on one side and a group of giggling girls on the other, when Hope walked over.

"Will you scoot over a bit so I can join you?" she asked.

Daniel started to move, but I just looked at her and, as loudly as I could, I told her, "No. I don't want to sit by you. I don't want to have anything to do with you ever again!" The hurt look in her eyes shot right through me. But I wasn't going to back down. I had to do this.

"But...but I thought we were... Don't you like me?" she stuttered.

I laughed right in her face. "Why would I like you?

Why would anyone like you? You're ugly, and stupid, and fat, and..." She ran off before I could say anything more.

Daniel went after her. He told me that, when he found her, she was in the corner of the gym, crying. When I saw her later that day, her eyes were red and she wouldn't look my way. That was the last time she ever spoke to me.

Kids can be so mean. Even kids who know better, who've been picked on themselves. They can still turn around and hurt others. I hurt someone once. A lot. And I never said I was sorry. But I am. If I could go back in time, if I could take back those words, I would do it in an instant. It would have been better to go through all the pain of being teased myself, rather than know that I caused that pain for someone else. Why did I do that? How could I do that?

Laura Birch

All day at school, my mind has been wandering. The kids are really having trouble paying attention and so am I. Maybe it's a full moon or something. My mind is just not on teaching.

I really hate when I have those days, those days when I know I'm not being the best teacher I can be. I try hard to live up to my own ideals of what a teacher should be. But I can't always do it. Once in a great while, I have a day where everything works just like I planned it, where the kids are excited and paying attention to what I have to say, and what I'm saying comes out just the way I want it to. These are the moments we teachers live for. And they are very rare, indeed. Most of the time, we just do the best we can, trying to keep afloat, and finally go home, hoping we can do better tomorrow.

I'm glad when the day is over, and I don't have to pretend my mind is on the present. Because really, it isn't. It's back with thirteen-year-old Laura, when I was a middle-school student and my parents started fighting.

I know that all parents fight sometimes, I write to Jacob when I'm able to sit down and add to the letter, *and some parents fight a lot worse than mine ever did. They never hurt each other physically, at least. But the verbal fighting... I think somehow, that was harder to take. Physical scars eventually heal and go away. Emotional ones never do.*

Even as a kid, I knew what they were fighting about— or at least I thought I knew. Money. There was never enough. Now don't get me wrong. We weren't poor. There were a lot of people much worse off than we were. But no matter how much money we had, it was never enough—never would be enough. Now I understand that my parents were always trying to fill a hole they had in their marriage, and in themselves. As a teenager, all I knew was that we needed money and we didn't have enough. And I knew that eating cost money.

Which is probably why I quit eating.

I know, that doesn't make much sense, but that's how I explained it to myself. After all, the money we saved on food could be used for more important things—like making my parents happy again.

Really, I think it was more a way to deal with all my conflicting emotions. I was worried about my parents. I wanted them to be happy. But I was also angry with them for putting me in that situation, for making me feel guilty for every penny I spent. And maybe I was trying to get their attention. Whatever the reason, not eating was something that I could control, in a world I felt I had very little control of.

Even at thirteen, I knew what anorexia was. We had a speaker come to our school to talk about eating disorders once. And of course, there were always the after school specials. But I never thought of myself as being anorexic.

After all, I ate sometimes, when people were watching me. And I never made myself throw up. But when people weren't watching over me, when I was supposed to "fend for myself" for dinner, I usually just skipped it altogether. And I didn't bother with lunch... or breakfast.

I didn't need to eat. I didn't feel like I deserved to eat. And most importantly, I didn't really feel like anyone cared if I ate or not. I guess that's the real reason I did it. My parents, and everyone else around me, were much more concerned with their own problems. They didn't have time to think about me or my needs. So I wouldn't think about my needs, either. Maybe that would show them!

I don't know what I thought I would "show them" by not eating. Maybe, if I starved myself enough, I'd end up in the hospital. Then they'd have to pay attention to me.

There may have been better ways to get attention, but at the time, I couldn't see any.

Jacob North

When Dad gets home, he is not happy. Despite all the chores I did while he was gone, all he sees is what I didn't get done. "I told you to clean the garage," he says. "Have you just been slacking all day?"

I don't bother pointing out the things I did get done. It would only get him more upset. He'd accuse me of "sassing back" to him. Whenever I say anything in my own defense, he says I'm sassing back. Be quiet and take the blame is what I've learned. He yells at me less that way. And the less he yells, the sooner I can get back to writing my letter.

Here comes the hardest part to talk about, I write as soon as Dad finishes dinner and goes upstairs. *The story of Daniel.*

I always knew that Daniel was a bit different from other kids. Personally, I liked his differences. For one thing, he wasn't afraid to be himself, to like the things he liked, even when nobody else did (or at least, when nobody else would admit to it.) He was fun and outgoing and full of life. He was also gay.

I think I knew it from the moment I met him. It didn't matter to me. He was a great friend, someone I enjoyed being around, and someone who would let me just be me. No games. No being mean to people I really liked. No trying to dress like everyone else, act like everyone else, be like everyone else. I could be myself.

But even though I knew he was gay, Daniel didn't really know (or wasn't able to admit it to himself) until we were freshmen in high school. By that point, his "differences" became more obvious. Kids started teasing him about it. Finally one day, he came out to me. He asked my advice on what to do.

Jacob North

I told him to be open about it. I told him to tell his parents and not to deny it to anyone. I knew he couldn't live his whole life trying to hide who he was from the world. I know the advice I gave him was good. And yet, I still wish I could take it all back, tell him that he should hide the truth, that he should just try to conform like everyone else. Not because I think he would have been happier that way, but because then he might still be...

Daniel officially came out in January of our freshman year. His parents were wonderful about it. They always loved him for who he was. The students at school (and even some of the teachers) were not. He had been teased a bit before, but now, the teasing was off the charts. The things they'd say to him...

"What are you looking at, faggot?"

"What's wrong with you, homo?"

Instead of saying, "Man, this is so gay" like some kids do when they don't like something, they created a new saying: "This is so Daniel!" The teacher would give us an assignment they didn't like, and they would complain. "Why do we have to do this? This is so Daniel. I mean, really?" And some of the teachers would laugh about it, even when Daniel was in the room.

Through it all, he put up with the teasing. He held his head up high and didn't let them get him down. (Okay, at least he didn't show them that they were getting him down. When no one else was around, he told me the truth about how much what they said hurt him, how he didn't know how much more he could take.)

Then they started beating him up. They'd wait for him after school, when he was walking home, then a group of them would jump him. Or they'd do it at school. As soon as the teacher left the room for a minute, they'd punch him. Or they'd try to catch him when he was in the bathroom.

I knew it was happening, but there wasn't much I could do about it. I couldn't follow him around all the time to guard him. And honestly, I wasn't much of a guard anyway. If they wanted, they could just beat me up, too.

He started skipping school a lot. And even when he was there, it was almost like he wasn't. He didn't talk much anymore, even to me. It was like he was pulling away from everything, lost in his own tortured world.

I should have tried harder to reach out. I shouldn't have let him pull away from me. I should have made him talk to me. I should have forced him to get help. I didn't know what to do. I didn't know how to reach him. But I should have tried.

I knew there were people who'd think about ending it. I've even seen kids with dull red lines or even scars on their arms, but I never really thought twice about it. Now I do.

On February 21st, at 2 o'clock in the morning, Daniel slashed his wrists. By the time someone found him, he was dead.

I have to stop writing because I can't see the page through my tears. Why had I decided to write this stupid letter? Why had I stopped to think about the past? And why, oh why, couldn't I go back and do things differently?

"Daniel," I whisper to the air. "I'm so sorry. I

should have done something... I should have..." I sniff. "Dammit."

Laura Birch

At school, Hope is beginning to drive me crazy. She always wants to be right next to me. Don't get me wrong: I like the girl. I try to do whatever I can to help her. But she's so needy. I don't think she gets enough attention from her parents, because she's always so eager to get it from anyone else she can. I try to help, but sometimes, it's hard to give it to her, especially in a week like this, when my mind's already so scattered.

By the time class is over, I just need a moment to myself before the next class comes in. But she doesn't leave. All the other kids file out, but she just stands there, waiting.

"Don't you have a class you need to go to, Hope?"

"I need to talk to you," she replies, then just stands there some more, looking at me.

She clearly needs me to start the conversation, whatever it's about. "What is it, Hope? You know you can tell me, right?"

She smiles. "Do you like me, Ms. Birch? Am I your favorite student?"

"You are one of my absolute favorites," I reply, purposely being a little bit vague.

"I'm sorry to tell you this, but I have to leave school," she says.

"For the day?"

"No. Forever. I've got to drop out. I'm gonna have a baby!" When she says that last part, she breaks out into a big smile.

What should I say? "Congratulations" never seemed to be the right reply when a teenage girl said she was expecting. "I'm sorry" would be more honest. But she is so happy. It is not my job to burst her bubble. Life will do that soon enough. "Oh," I say, instead. "Um...When are you due?" What else was I going to say? She doesn't look pregnant yet, but Hope always did have a little bit of extra weight on her, so it would be a while before a bump would be noticeable.

"In July. Maybe she'll be born on July 4th and she can be my little USA baby. I can dress her up in red, white, and blue and stars and everything."

I want to shake her, to tell her that she's not talking about getting a doll. This is a real person she's bringing into the world. She'll be responsible for it for the rest of her life.

But a lecture isn't going to do her any good now. All I can do was offer her support. "Do you already know if it's a girl?"

"Well, I don't officially know yet," she says as she rubs her stomach. "I'm getting an ultrasound next week. But I just know she's going to be a cute little baby girl."

I think about that little girl and wonder if she'll end up like her mother, ignored and so eager for attention that she'll do almost anything to get it. Even get herself pregnant at sixteen.

Or will it go the other way? Will she be smothered by a mother who thought her child could give her all the love she was never able to get anywhere else?

And then I wonder if I'll be her teacher sixteen years from now, seeing first-hand the effects of her mother's decisions. And I wonder if there's anything I can do to stop this cycle.

I think about Hope again later, as I sit down to finish my letter to Jacob. I think about her and about all the students I've had over the years, all the kids who needed help, more help than I could ever give them. Why had I ever decided to become a teacher?

I have fought with depression all of my life, I write to Jacob that night. *By high school, it really got bad. Of course, I never told anyone about it. What could I say? And what could they do if I told them? But inside, I* was always hoping someone would notice, that someone would see my pain and make it go away.

I still have notebooks from when I was in high school, with pages covered in writing. Things like:

"I hate life."

"Nobody cares."

"What would it matter?"

"I can't do this anymore."

"Stop the pain."

"Help!"

I wrote this all over my notebooks, in the middle of class. But no one ever noticed it. I was the good student, the quiet student. I didn't cause anyone trouble. So no one ever noticed me. No one ever reached out a hand to help me. And I, alone in my misery, was never able to ask for help.

Obviously, I didn't kill myself. I never even tried. But I thought about it all the time. Dreamed about how I would do it, about how everyone else would react once they found out. But I didn't have the strength to do anything about it, any more than I had the strength to ask for help. I just kept it all inside. And did my best to get through another day.

They say it's normal for teens to go through a time where they think about death, about killing themselves. I don't know if it's "normal," but I do know that it's awful, and I wouldn't wish it on anybody.

When I decided to become a teacher, my goal, more than anything else, was to help students who were having a hard time–students like me. I wanted to be there, to make their lives better, to let them know that they were not alone in the world. I didn't realize, when I started, how many students there are like that. Or how hard it would be to help them. But even now, I keep trying.

I told you when I started this letter that I was sorry about what happened. And I'll say it again, now. I didn't mean to get you into trouble. I wanted to help you. I wanted to be the person that I always dreamed of when I was your age–the one who saw the pain and reached out a hand to help.

I read a quote once that I've tried to live by ever since: "Always be kinder than necessary because everyone you *meet is fighting some kind of battle." This is so true. I've seen so many students fighting so many battles. All I can do is try my best to be "kinder than necessary," to reach out a hand to them and hope they take it.*

I want to help you, Jacob. I don't know how. I don't know if you'll even let me. But if nothing else, I want you to know that you are not alone.

Laura Birch

Jacob North

"Are you finished with that letter yet?" my dad asks me, as a way of waking me up. "I told her you would have it done by Friday morning. That's tomorrow."

"Not yet," I mumble and pull my covers back over my head.

My dad grabs the covers and yanks them off me. "Today's your last day to work on it. It will be done by the time I get home from work."

"Okay, okay," I reply.

"And you're going to have to take it to the school tomorrow morning. I was going to do it, but I can't get off from work. I have a big meeting I have to be at. Just take it to the office and tell them who it's for. They can't complain about you being at school long enough to do that."

Whew! I'd forgotten that Dad had said he was going to take the note in. If he had read it...

"Okay, Dad. I'll take care of it," I tell him, trying not to sound too relieved. I don't want him to start wondering why I didn't want him to see it.

Once he leaves, I start on the final story. My life now.

Things have been difficult ever since Daniel died, I write. I don't get picked on anymore and I get along okay with my classmates. But I don't really have any friends, either. I mostly just keep to myself.

Which means I keep my feelings to myself, too. When I'm feeling lonely, or angry, or sad, or all three at the same time... Sometimes, I write about it. Other times, I cut myself.

Yeah, I know that cutting is bad. Yeah, I know I shouldn't do it. But sometimes...I don't know... What else is there to do? *The anger builds up inside me. There's no way to let it escape. Except with a blade on my skin.*

It started out small. Just a small scratch on my wrist. But each time, I need to do more and more. About a month ago, I cut the word HATE in big letters down my arm. If my dad ever paid attention to me, he would have seen it. But he doesn't and he didn't. I got a few odd looks from a couple kids at school, but even still, nobody said anything to me about it.

But lately, I've been trying really hard not to cut, because honestly, I'm afraid one of these days I'll go too far. So when I get the urge to pull out my knife, I grab a pencil instead and start to write. If I can get my feelings down on paper, perhaps I can release them that way. Maybe I won't need the blood.

Which leads me to your question, Ms. Birch. You asked me why I wrote that note. I wrote that note, with a pencil on paper, because if I hadn't, I would have written it in blood, on my skin, instead. I wrote that note because I'm trying to save myself.

I don't want to end up like Daniel.

YANA [You Are Not Alone]

I want to live.

And that is why I wrote that note.

Jacob North

Laura Birch

I leave for school early the next morning. I don't know when Jacob's father is going to drop off the letter and I want to make sure my letter is ready and waiting when he gets there.

I leave my letter, in a sealed envelope, with the secretary. I'm a bit worried about letting it out of my possession. To be honest, I don't want it to fall into the wrong hands. It is rather personal, after all. But I want to make sure Jacob gets it before his Code of Conduct meeting that afternoon.

I've already decided that I'm going to be at that meeting. I don't have to be. The teachers involved usually aren't. But I have a few things I want to say.

I'm not going to let Jacob be expelled for this. At least, not if I can help it.

So I drop off the letter in the office and then do my best to be a good teacher, to focus on the students who are present, for the rest of the day. I'm not sure how well I succeed, but I do the best I can. I guess that's all we can ever really do.

Jacob North

I take my letter for Ms. Birch in to the school first thing in the morning. Dad gave me specific instructions to go straight to the office, give it to a secretary, and then come home. I'm not supposed to "stop and talk to my friends." My dad doesn't even know that I don't really have any friends. Not since Daniel...

I don't expect there to be anything waiting for me when I get there. But when I hand the secretary my letter, sealed tight in an envelope to protect it from curious eyes, she hands me one in return.

"This is from Ms. Birch," she says. "She wanted me to make sure this got to you."

I take the envelope she's holding. It's thick.

"What's in here?" I ask, but the secretary just shrugs and goes back to her work.

I don't go back home. I'd been stuck in that house all week. Dad said I couldn't stick around the school, but he didn't say I couldn't go anywhere else.

Instead, I go to the park near my house. There's still snow on the ground, but the sun is shining through the clouds. I can smell spring in the air.

I brush the snow off a park bench and sit down. It's still a bit cold out, but the sun feels so good on my face, after this long winter, that I'm not going to let the cold get to me.

I open the envelope and stare, surprised, at the pages inside. It's a letter, hand-written, from Ms. Birch. It's not a letter accusing me of being a bad kid, of saying mean things about her. No. The letter starts, *Dear Jacob, I want you to know that I am very sorry about what happened today. I did not mean to get you into trouble. All I wanted to do was help you...*

Laura Birch

During my prep time, I go down to the office to see if Jacob's dad had left a letter for me. He might not have. He might not have it done yet. He might have forgotten all about it. But I have to check, just to make sure.

Jacob's letter is there, waiting for me. A big letter in a sealed envelope. I guess I'm not the only one who has a lot to say.

I take it back to my classroom, close and lock the door, and sit down to read.

Dear Ms. Birch, You want to know why I wrote that note? Okay, I'll tell you why I wrote it. But I want you to ask yourself this: Do you really want to know?

Yes, I do. I want to know everything I can.

It takes me all hour to read. It's the best use of my prep time I've ever had.

And as I'm reading, I come up with an idea. I suddenly know what I can do to turn this situation into something positive. I finally see a way I can help students who feel like they are all alone in the world. I'm ready for this meeting—I've never been more ready for a meeting in my whole career.

Jacob North

My dad makes me get all dressed up for the Code of Conduct hearing, like I'm going to a real court or something. He left work early so he could be there, too, to keep up the image of the good dad.

Actually, I'm glad he's going to be there. To be honest, I'm a bit scared. Having him by my side is comforting.

"Thanks for being here with me," I tell him.

He looks at me, surprised. Come to think of it, I don't think I say thank you to him very much. Maybe I should start doing it more. After all, he is doing his best to raise me, and that can't always be easy.

"Of...of course," he replies. "It's my job to be here for you."

I smile. He is doing the best he can, I just forget sometimes. "I love you, Dad," I tell him. Again, he gives me that look of surprise. I guess I'm just full of surprises today.

"I love you, too, Jacob," he replies. "Don't ever forget that."

The hearing itself goes pretty quickly. It consists of Mr. Jones, the principal, two other teachers that I recognize but have never had, and Ms. Birch. I didn't realize she was going to be there. When I look at her, she gives me an encouraging smile. I smile back. No matter what happens at this hearing, I know I now have at least one friend at this school.

Mr. Jones tells the council what my offense is. The other teachers ask him a few questions. Nobody addresses me.

"Well," Mr. Jones says, "I think, considering

the nature of the threat... I mean, we can't have kids talking about teachers like this...we have to expel him. We need to send a message that this will not be tolerated."

That's when Ms. Birch pipes up. "Mr. Jones, can I speak for a moment?"

Mr. Jones looks at her, confused. She obviously wasn't following the normal protocol. "I...I suppose so. After all, the threat was to you."

"I understand that you don't want Jacob to get away with what he did without some kind of punishment. Right?"

Mr. Jones nods his head and motions for her to continue.

"Well," Ms. Birch begins, tentatively. "As far as having to send a message to the other students... the kids don't know what happened. They will just know that Jacob is suddenly no longer in school. I'm not sure how that is sending a message."

Mr. Jones scowls. "Well, I, um... It's the principle of the thing, you see."

"But if instead of expelling him, we keep him at school, maybe give him a more public punishment..."

"Like what? Janitor duty?"

Ms. Birch shakes her head. I can tell she's picking her words carefully. Even I know it's risky for her to challenge Mr. Jones like this. She's really putting her neck out for me. "I have a suggestion for something I think that might be more appropriate."

"I'm listening," Mr. Jones says, but he doesn't seem too happy about it.

"I want to start an after school group for students—kind of a support group for students who are struggling with difficult times. As punishment for what he did, I think Jacob should have to help me with this group." Ms. Birch gives me a smile. "That would send a message to the students that you can't threaten teachers with impunity. And Jacob would be giving back to the school. Kind of like doing community service."

"Well, I..." Mr. Jones stutters. "I mean... This would be a volunteer position, Ms. Birch. You know there's no room in the budget for extra pay for after school activities."

Ms. Birch smiles. "I know. But I want to do it."

Mr. Jones looks at the other teachers, who nod. "Well, then, I...I guess we're all in agreement. Jacob will not be expelled, but he will be required to assist you, in any way you need, with starting this new after school group for... what are you going to call this group, Ms. Birch?"

"I don't know. I haven't decided yet."

That's when I speak up. I'm not sure if I'm supposed to say anything at my own hearing, but I have a spark of inspiration I just need to share. "Let's call it the YANA Club. YANA for You Are Not Alone. Our goal will be, like that quote says, 'to be kinder than necessary to others who are fighting their own battles.'"

"Perfect," Ms. Birch agrees.

And that is how the first chapter of The YANA Club is founded.

Laura Birch

There are more kids at the first meeting of The YANA Club than I expect. I guess Jacob isn't the only one who is going through some rough times. I knew that, but I'm still surprised by how many kids are willing to admit they need some help, and at how many students feel alone.

The first thing we do is write "letters of remembering." I want each kid to take a moment and think about someone else who is fighting a battle, someone who they can reach out to and help through a hard time.

I write to Daniel. Reading about Daniel from Jacob's point of view reminded me of what it felt like when I found out that he was dead. He'd been one of my students when it happened. He was one of the few bright spots in a really rough school year for me. I had looked forward to seeing his smiling face each day...

Dear Daniel,

I am so sorry about all the struggles you went through in your life. I wish I could have done something to help you, before it was too late. I knew things were a bit difficult for you, but I had no idea how hard they really were. And for that, I am truly sorry.

I will never forget your struggle to be true to yourself. I will try, for the rest of my life, to be on the lookout for those in pain, to help everyone I can, as much as I can. It will not bring you back, but perhaps it will help ensure that your death was not in vain.

Laura Birch

Jacob North

Ms. Birch has us start off our meeting by writing a "letter of remembering." First, I think about writing to Daniel. I will always remember and miss him.

Then, I think maybe I should write to Brandon. I heard last week that he'd been sent to jail. Nobody knew the specifics, but they said it had to do with his mom and her boyfriend. Despite everything he'd put me through, I realize now that I feel sorry for him. He obviously has a few battles of his own to fight.

But instead, I write this:

Dear Hope,

I heard that you're leaving school and why. I'd like

to say I am happy for you, but honestly, I am just sad that you won't be here anymore. But more than that, I am really feeling sorry for hurting you so long ago. I never should have treated you that way, and I wish I could go back and change it now.

I want you to know that, no matter what your future brings, you are not alone. If you ever need a friend, I will always be here for you.

And I will be kinder than necessary.

Jacob North

Thank you so much for reading my book!

If this book touched you, inspired you, or
just gave you something to think about, please
recommend it to someone else you think might
appreciate it, too. Please help spread the message
that You Are Not Alone!

If you liked it, you can find my other titles
and, hopefully, leave a positive review at
www.enchantmentpress.com and/or amazon.com.
Your good words mean a lot
to independent authors.

If you have any suggestions to make it better, please
send an email to enchantmentpress@gmail.com.

Made in the USA
Middletown, DE
28 February 2023

25761085R00060